Almoose Asleep

Bearly Awake

D0817429

THIS BOOK BELONGS TO:

Name: _____

PHONE: _____

LAZY one.

Bearly Awake

Almoose Asleep

Almoose Asleep

Bearly Awake

For my "grandpappy bears," who always believed in me:

Grandpa L. Gail Johnson, who (repeatedly!) told me I should write children's books, and
Grandpa DelMar A. Higham, who asked me to write "funny letters" to make him chuckle.

Love and miss you more than I can say.
-J.H.L.

For Tyson and Lily and Grace with all my heart.
You make me happy.

-G.W.B.

Copyright ©2014 LazyOne, Inc. All Rights Reserved.
No part of this publication can be reproduced without
permission from LazyOne. Blah blah blah blah blah blah....
For permission contact LazyOne, Inc.
3065 N. 200 W., North Logan, Utah 84341

ISBN: 978-0-9851005-4-4

Printed in China

LazyOne, Inc.
Timbuktu, Madagascar, Bronx
Fargo, Little Rock, Tijuana, Siberia.

Bearly Awake
and Almoose Asleep

By Jenny H. Lyman
Illustrated by Gideon Burnett

Way up in pine country where the big river flows
There's a sweet fishing spot where a bear family goes.
And all summer long those big bears go about
Stuffing their faces with berries and trout.

But when it turns cold, Ole Grandpappy Bear
Rises up on his feet and he roars through the air:
"Hup-ho, family! It's time to forget this fiesta!
Let's tromp to our dens for a good, long siesta!"

So the bear family lumbers on up to their lair,
They brush all their teeth and they comb all their hair.
They put on their sleep clothes with flaps in the backs
And snuggle deep into their cozy sleep sacks.

But Bear's just not ready. He wants some more lunch!
He craves fish and pine nuts and tubers that crunch!
So amid all the dozing and sleeping and snoring
Bear sneaks to the river for further exploring.

"I'm nowhere *near* sleepy!" Bear firmly protests.
So he fishes and gathers and happ'ly taste-tests.
BUT...Bear has forgotten his "snoozity beeper,"
(The internal clock that will *make* him a sleeper).

Thus, precisely at sunset, as Bear eats a trout,
His "snoozity" beeps...and Bear plumb
ZONKS OUT.

With a great big kerPLOP he falls right in that stream!
And nothing can wake him—he's starting to dream.

Poor Bear is quite stuck, and his feast's at an end.

But lucky for him, he has Moose for a friend!

Moose hears the kerPLOP and he groans. "OH TARNATION!

Bear's stuck in the river for his hibernation!"

"**I** must get him home to his family lair—
A river's no place for a big, snoring bear!
I've got to just think about this. Hey—I know!
I'll push Bear back home in my big wheel-bear-oh!"

Well, it takes mighty effort. Moose lifts, lugs and drags,
And when Bear is all loaded, my, how that cart sags!
They make it downriver 'bout—oh—fifty yards,
Then the wheel-bear-oh bursts into slivers and shards.

"OH PHOOEY!" yells Moose, "My cart is now junk!"
He sits there and stews—then along comes a skunk.

See, Skunk is not pleased by the loud interruption.
He takes aim at Moose and prepares for...

eruption!

The blast is so stinky, Moose runs for the trees—
And catches his antlers on hives of mad bees.
Now dripping with honey, Moose shoves and he heaves
That great lug of a bear through the grass and the leaves.

"**T**he leaves are all sticking!" Moose tries to be brave.
"But I've got to keep moving! Bear still needs his cave."

So, with great perseverance, up hills and 'round bends,
Moose keeps pushing Bear until the trail...ends!

And looking around him, Moose sees—oh *HOORAY!*
Bear's family den is just three feet away!
Bear wakes with a start. "Well, Moose! Say, you're tardy!
'Bout time you showed up to my long slumber party!"

"You'll never believe all the dreams that I've had—
Rivers and beehives, and smells that were bad...
And um, Moose? No offense, but you look sorta funny!
Why did you dress up in fall leaves and sweet honey?"

Moose just rolls his eyes, and Bear yawns a great yawn.
"Let's go nap!" Moose replies as they're crossing the lawn.
The friends enter the cave and collapse in a heap—
Bearly awake, and almoose asleep!

Other books with matching pajamas
available from LazyOne:

Duck Duck Moose

Pasture Bedtime